The Narc that I know

By
Catherine Glover

Table of Contents

Intro

Christina was in her mid-40s when she started to come into her own. She has so much love in her heart and in her soul. She thought she knew how to love or what love truly was or did. Until one day she met a man who would teach her the true meaning of love but not in a positive way.

Being with Timothy taught her many lessons. They had more than a bond, it was a soul tie.

Ultimately they found out that it was more than a soul tie the connection was so strong. They're always going to be connected, they are twin flames. It's very rare that you meet your twin flame in this lifetime. This narcissistic, karmic toxic bond was part of their destiny. There was a higher calling in both of their lives.

Chapter One

Who is He

In September 2015, I received a check that my mother left me after she passed away. This gave me enough money to get my own place and move to the city. The city of Trenton New Jersey. This was the one city that I did not want to move to. But it was close to my job at the time and the only thing I could get with my credit score. By the way, I'm Christina Williams, but you can call me Tina for short. Ironically my middle name is Marie. As in the R&B singer Teena Marie. She spells Tina differently though. People always thought it was cute to call me Tina Marie instead of just Tina. I'm not mad about that at all, She's one of my favourite singers. I love her and all of her music. Especially her song that she did with Rick James called Fire and Desire. That song perfectly describes how I felt when I met "The Pain of My Life".

I am a Registered nurse at RWJ Hospital and have been for twenty - two years now. A coworker of mine named Jennifer Mays told me about a house right next door to her that was for rent. So she had got the number for me. I quickly got in touch with the landlord and was able to put down a deposit. The place was not available until October of that year. Which was fine since I was staying with a relative at the time. The house was painted a funny colour green on the outside with white trimmings. Very small but had three bedrooms, two baths, an upstairs, a front porch and a backyard. Just enough for me and my kids, John and Stacey. It was on a quiet one-way street named Chaplin Street. Right in the middle of a bad neighborhood. But it was what I could afford at the time. Besides it was next to my coworker's house. She and I became real close, she was like a sister to me. Once I moved in, Jennifer and I began going to the casino on a regular basis. A lot of times we went straight after getting off work at six o'clock in the morning. We worked nights and on the weekends at the hospital. I didn't mind that shift, however, I feared for my kids being home at night in that neighborhood. I knew this would be temporary until something better came along. So we made the best of it. Not too long after I moved next to my coworker, she moved to another house down the street. Jennifer had one boy, but he was a teenager so she needed a two-bedroom. The house they stayed in next to me only had one bedroom. We were pretty close. I considered her to be a real friend. However, later down the road, she let me know that I was completely wrong about that. One day, the following summer, I went down to her house just to hang out for a little bit because it was our night off. I didn't know she had company.

It was this guy named Scrappy from across the street. Scrappy wasn't his real name of course. He adopted that name in his teenage years because he was always fighting. So they started calling him Scrappy because he loved to "Scrap". His real name is Timothy James Butler. He lived directly across the street from Jennifer, with his mom, daughter, son and one of his brothers. This was my first time meeting him. He was actually sleeping on her couch when I came in. Jennifer introduced us and we began chatting. During this time I was 3 years single. I also was in my, I don't want to say, 304 (hoe) phase.. but anyway, let's call it what it is. I recall saying to him since he was sleeping, would you like to sleep with me in my bed sometime? You would never believe that I was shy and insecure with a statement like that. He smiled and said anything was possible. We both looked at each other and laughed. He was a nice Simi muscular chocolate man, with a lot of tattoos and a nice smile. Once he stood up I could see that he was slightly taller than me. He had on this florescent yellow and green worker vest. I thought he might have worked for the sanitation department or did construction or something. Later on, I found out that he was actually doing community service that day. But I didn't care, I was just trying to have a friends-with-benefits type situation with him. We talked for maybe an hour and I excused myself because I had to go home and start dinner. So I said it was nice to meet you and maybe we'll see each other again someday. I left the house and as I was walking to my house I heard somebody behind me talking. It was Scrappy he was following me to my house. I thought to myself, "Well damn he's quite persistent, giving off" thirsty AF vibes" I'm not even gonna front, I thought it was kinda cute. So he walked me to my front door we exchanged numbers and

He said, "I'm going to call you later". I said yeah you do that. Unfortunately, I didn't hear from him till maybe a couple of days later but it was still okay because we had no commitment to one another. Besides I didn't want to seem thirsty and he probably didn't want to seem thirsty either. He called me Friday morning and said he wanted to take me out that night. I agreed to it because this was the start of my three-week vacation. Scrappy took me to a local bar where they played old-school hip-hop music. We danced. I was excited because I haven't been out on a real date in a long time plus I was horny. The way he looked at me, he could have undressed me with his eyes. I don't know, there's something sexy about a guy who looks at you like he wants to sex you up real bad. That is a complete turn-on. Clearly, this guy knew I wanted the same thing because after all that dancing, his dick was on READY and we both were ready to go.

Scrappy practically knew everyone who came in that night. Of course he did, this was his hood. He introduced me as his lady friend. I admired him for that. We had a good time that night. We stayed until the last call. Then we went back to my place. Surely you can guess what happened next. We kissed at the front door. He grabbed me to pull me closer to him. Softly kissing my neck. While running his two large hands up and down my back. Then he kissed my lips with the slowest passion ever. Needless to say, I was beginning to get extremely aroused. Once he moved those big soft hands across my breast, ooooh chile it was over! I took him upstairs to my bedroom. We couldn't keep our hands off of each other. He continued to kiss my neck and began to undress me. I had on a spaghetti-strapped red baby doll dress. He took my straps down one by one, kissing each shoulder with those juicy succulent lips. Once he got my dress off, he pushed me down on the bed. Now those juicy lips were kissing and sucking on my large breast., in the middle and all around. His long tongue ran straight down the middle of my chest past my belly button, all the way down to my clitoris. He quickly pulled my panties off. Now I'm getting the full effect of that strong-mouth game. I thought I had died and gone to heaven. Lord, what is this man doing to me? Once he was done eating my box, he raised my ass higher so he could devour the juices that ran down my anus. This was the first time ever that anyone has licked my asshole. It was phenomenal.

Now that he had me in the right position, it was time for Jimmy to enter into my hot, throbbing, juicy fruit. For those of you who don't know who or what Jimmy is, I suggest you go to the urban dictionary or ask the rapper KRS One. Did I mention that this man knew exactly what he was doing? Baebee, the best sex I've had in years.

He spent the night with me and in the morning we went out to Breakfast at a dinner across the bridge. When I say across the bridge that means going into the next state which was Pennsylvania. It only took ten minutes to get there. This place was more like a small deli, where you could dine in or take out. We chose to dine in. I ordered the French toast with pork bacon and scrambled eggs with cheese. He ordered a ham and cheese omelette with a side of potatoes. The food and the conversation were good. It was a good feeling being in the company of a man after being single for three years and not really getting out to date. So it was exciting. During breakfast, Scrappy said to me, that he might have to snatch me up because he felt I was good for him. He wanted me to himself. I smiled and at that moment I was feeling him too. But I did not let him know that at that time. For me, I was just having fun and didn't want to rush anything. I felt like I barely knew him which I didn't. I wanted to leave my options open. We left there to go back home. He parked in front of my house. We kissed and went our separate ways

Chapter Two

A Fools Playground

Summertime of August 2016 I remember this time because I was actually talking to another young man named Andre. I met him a year ago online. We belonged to the same Facebook group. We became real good friends. He told me he was staying in Chicago I never thought about having a long-distance relationship but for some reason, I was drawn to this person. When I finally did meet "Dre", it was a complete nightmare. The first time he came to see me was when I was staying with my cousin Barbara after my mom passed away. Andre decided to take the Greyhound bus to where I stayed with my cousin.

First of all, what was supposed to be a ten-hour bus ride turned into an eighteen-hour bus ride for him. The driver got lost and somehow they ended up in the mountains in Pennsylvania. Once they found their way back to the highway the bus broke down. They had to wait three hours for a replacement bus. Anything that you could imagine that could go wrong definitely went wrong. It was the bus ride from hell. His whole trip to get to me was a disaster. Once he made it here, my cousin was not feeling him at all. She has a knack for reading people or getting certain Vibes from them. I'm not saying that she is always right but the vibe she got when she met him, she was right on the money. Once he arrived at the house, I went upstairs to finish getting ready for our date. So my cousin had time to sit there and talk with him. They talked for maybe about thirty minutes. When I was finally ready, I came downstairs my cousin pulled me aside in the kitchen. She said that man is full of shit. He uses women for money. Now when I tell you I was taking back by those words, I was not completely in disbelief. I was just thrown off because how could she tell that by just having one conversation with him? Am I that naive and desperate to not realize what he was up to? Yes, I had sent him money a few times and people were telling me a woman should never send or give a man any money, especially somebody she just met on the internet. But me being stupid, naive or just wanting to be loved, seems like I would fall for anything and everything. My cousin Barbara was completely right about him. Unfortunately, I had to find that out the hard way. The reason why he had such a terrible time getting to me was nothing but God telling him that you're not about the play with my child.

I didn't know it then but I know it now.

I took him around to meet my family because I thought he was a cool person. Although I was keeping my options open, Andre had a pretty good chance of being my man. I was entertaining the idea of him being my man Even though it would have been a long-distance relationship. I had met him before I met Scrappy. So I was talking to him while I was seeing Scrappy. Again I had to leave my options open. I wasn't really settling down for anything but I thought Andre had a good chance. So that was the first time he came down. Two weeks later, after Scrappy stayed the night at my house. Andre came to my house on Chaplin Street. We had discussed him possibly moving in with me. Then I received a strange text message. It was a really long message that appeared to be from my aunt's cell phone number. Honestly, it must have been my mother texting from the heavens above, saying how disappointed she was in me and don't be stupid don't be a fool. It was very scrambled, so I couldn't make out the whole entire message. I asked my aunt why she sent me this message and why it looked like that. She said I didn't send you a message! That was definitely my Mother messaging me about Andre.

Basically not trust him it was the craziest thing I had ever seen. I have never experienced anything like that.

Andre came down from Chicago I took him to meet my girlfriend Jennifer who lived up the street. And this time her friend Raniequa was over there. They called her Rah Rah for short. Raniequa was very pretty. But the problem with her was she likes drama. She likes to fight and cause all kinds of chaos. Rah was always getting into a fight with somebody. She's the type of person who if it's quiet in the neighborhood, she'll create some drama. She was definitely for the streets. Andre and I sat down at the table... they wanted to play spades. I just wanted to watch because I didn't know how to play. Yes this black girl from Bensalem PA did not know how to play spades. Y'all can take away my black card later. I knew Andre would fit right in with them because he likes to get high and drink liquor just like they do. I'm sitting at the table with Andre and Raniequa Next thing I notice my friend Scrappy comes in. My mouth drops because I wasn't expecting him to come through. It's been two weeks since we've spent the night together. We said hello to each other and acted like we weren't messing around or anything because technically we went on one date. It wasn't a big deal at the time. Scrappy left ten minutes later. I thought to myself, did he just leave because I was with another guy? He can't be serious right now, we barely know each other. Thirty minutes go by, next thing I notice Scrappy comes back. This time he returns with a lady friend. I said oh wow now it's really awkward. His lady friend was faded real bad. She had on a torn blue mini skirt with a see-through white t-shirt, no bra on, so her nipples were showing. Her wig looked like she had it for twenty years. She immediately passed out on the couch. All I Could Do Was laugh to myself and think wow he really bought this chick over here, to do what, make me jealous? He looked like he grabbed her off the street corner to be honest I just sat there shaking my head as I sipped my alcoholic beverage that Jennifer made me drink. She said come on now, Tina you got to drink something. You can't sit there and be looking all dead when you are with us you got to drink something. When I tell you the peer pressure was real. I obliged but not too much. I didn't want to get completely drunk because I know how I am when I get that way. Besides my fling was in town and I wanted to spend time with him. So I didn't want to sit there drinking all night with them. But apparently, that's what he wanted to do. I was already having reservations about this guy. So I was conflicted. Could it have been because I was thinking about Scrappy the whole time I was sitting there and the way that he made me feel a couple of weeks ago? Scrappy and Andre ended up teaming up and they played against Rah and Jennifer. I sat there watching as I stated earlier. They played one game. Needless to say, the ladies won. Scrappy said he had to go take his friend home because she was completely passed out. Now I'm getting tired. Besides Andre just got here and I wanted to go back to the house and spend some time with him. He tells me he's not ready to go yet because he was having a good time. I ended up leaving him there because for me that's not a good time. I'm not going to continue to sit there and watch people play cards all night. I'm not even drinking like them so I wanted to leave. I was not comfortable, this wasn't my scene at all. No, I'm not bougie like Scrappy told me I was. We like what we like, that's it! I returned to my house and turned some reggae music on. Even though I was supposed to be with Andre that night, all I could think about was grinding with Scrappy while the beat was playing slow and steady.

An hour and a half goes by Andre still doesn't come back to the house. So now I'm calling him to see what the problem is.

I Started yelling at him over the phone, what's happening? Let's goooo! Who the hell comes from out of town to go spend time with your friends but not you? So disrespectful! I was already on the fence about this guy and I was getting tired of him. So he finally comes to the house. We argued about him being disrespectful and how disappointed I was. He apologized and now we're having sex. Now my mood is dead and nothing about his sex was impressive. It was nothing spectacular. This is a person who says he has fallen in love with me and wants to be with me. There's no real connection there. At this point, I'm so over Andre. Maybe I was thinking about Scrappy way too much.

Nah it was definitely Andre and the way he made me feel once he saw me. He was not a good dude. Turns out he was indeed a manipulator and a con artist. It was true that he hit females up for money. Because now I'm hearing from other women who were in the same group. Same scenario, that he went to see them. They were sending him money. Paying for tickets, buying him jewellery, buying him basically whatever he wanted. I really felt like such a fool. When I confronted him about it he basically cut me off he said he didn't want to hear from me any more and he's with this other girl now. He cut me off to go be with somebody else right in my face, I was devastated. I had to ask myself, "How could you let somebody do this to you?" Apparently, that would be my MO for my next set-up. My next relationship was very similar but a lot more elaborate. Like how I just allowed these guys to do whatever they wanted to to me and I did nothing about it. Yet I keep giving them every piece of me, every part of me, everything that their broken ass hearts desired. I kept pouring everything into them and they gave me nothing in return. Nothing but heartache, headaches, disrespect and disappointments. Lord knows that was one of the lessons that I had to learn throughout my whole life. Okay, now that I think I learned my lesson I can move on with my life.

So I thought... A week later after Andre went back to Chicago, I saw Scrappy again. This time he walked to my house with his dog Kels and his son Dashawn. This was my first time meeting them both. We stood outside talking and I ended up giving his son some animated DVDs to watch since my son was a lot older and I didn't need those DVDs anymore. A few moments later they went on to walk the dog and I went back in the house. Later on that night, Scrappy came over he stayed the night again. This time he stayed all day with me the next day I made breakfast we watched movies and we lay there just holding each other. He laid on his back looking at the ceiling and said it's so peaceful over here, I feel at peace. I know his life was just like any other Hood life I wouldn't say hectic but he didn't have a moment of peace. In my mind, he had to deal with whatever he had going on. Especially having to be a single father. I thought that was commendable that he had his son with him. All I knew about the baby mama at the time was she was an unfit parent and that he had just got custody of his son through DYFS. I didn't even want to know what made her lose her child like that. I didn't want to know at the time because I felt like it was none of my business. Like I said we weren't in a relationship so the less I knew about that aspect of his life I was content with it. I didn't want to know too much on that Spectrum at the time but now I wish I had asked the right questions at that time. Every day after that Scrappy came over we hung out we were getting pretty close so I asked him how he actually felt about me I asked him if he felt anything at all. Where would he like this to go? He said he feels something but he's not sure where he wants to go at this time. so I just left at that.

Jennifer is calling my phone. Sometimes she can be loud, obnoxious and somewhat demanding. She thinks the world revolves around her and that you need to do as she says not as she does. Frankly, I was getting a bit tired of her. She had already made a lot of enemies at work I was basically the only friend she had at work because she burned a lot of Bridges with everybody. Now she's asking me about her brother Scrappy. She considers Scrappy to be her brother because that's what they do around here call each other brother and sister but they're not actual brothers and sisters. So she asked me, what's going on with you with my brother? I said what do you mean? She was like he's spending a lot of time over there with you. Now I'm confused I'm looking at my phone like is this chick serious right now? So what he's spending a lot of time with me, I said. That's my business. She says, oh you not going to tell me? Then she proceeded to ask me how the dick is. First of all, I don't ask you about your Private Affairs, the two guys and the female that you're messing with at work at the same time. I do not ask you how the sex is with anyone that you are seeing. So what gives you the right to ask me about what's going on in my sex life? She said well I heard that Community dick is good AF, he got some good Community dick. This girl is on one right now. Why would I tell you that? I had to ask her, "Are you trying to fuck him or something"? Jennifer says, no that's wrong I'm messing with his brother. Oh on top of the three people at work? For some reason right then in there I knew she wanted to have sex with him. I asked Scrappy if they ever did anything before and are y'all currently fucking? Why is she so concerned about if you are with me or not? He said no we not doing anything, she wants to do something but she messing with my brother I'm not touching that. The next day Jennifer called me. This time she calls herself cussing me out for asking Scrappy about if they were fucking. Whose friend are you supposed to be right now? You mad at me for having a conversation with him? He went back and told Jennifer about the conversation he and I had. Now I'm looking at dude like are your serious right now, what game is this? This is some petty high school shit! I said to him, now that I know she wants to fuck you, I don't think it's a good idea for you to be at her house anymore. Especially if you want to still see me. This messy-ass dude goes back and tells this chic that I'm trying to control him. Man listens, when they say some guys gossip more than females, he was living proof of that.

Now I'm looking at him sideways. What's worse than that is, now Jennifer and I are getting into it about somebody neither one of us is in a relationship with. We're supposed to be homegirls. Now I'm starting to see why people don't mess with her. I remember telling my other coworker/ friend Mia, that I had to leave them toxic people alone and move off of that street. Days go by without talking to any of them. Scrappy came to my house and said he wanted to talk. No apology for the shit he did, we went straight to my bed.

Apparently, I have no self-control when it comes to him. In the morning we went to breakfast again. This time I drove. When we got back to my house, he walked me to my front door and kissed me. Then he proceeded to walk down the street to his house. I see Jennifer pull up on the side of him. She immediately started yelling at him because she wanted him to get her table that she left at my house. When she was in the process of moving down the street, she had to hurry to get out of the old house she was in. She didn't have time to move everything down so she put some stuff in my house. The table was the last thing she needed to pick up. When she saw Scrappy, she started yelling at him through her car window, "I could have sworn I asked you to do me a favor"! Scrappy frowned up his face because he had no idea what she was talking about or who she thought she was yelling at. Apparently, the day before she wanted him to get the table from out of my house and bring it down to her house. Because she and I weren't really talking at the time. So now she's yelling at him like he's one of her children I just closed the door because I'm not even getting into all of that nonsense. I don't understand why she just couldn't send her son to my house to get it if she wanted it that bad. People are just weird and are doing the most for no reason. I made up my mind right then and there that I was done with that chick for real. On another occasion I'm riding past the liquor store around the corner I see Raniequa and another girl walking by, so Rah yells at me as I'm riding by... "and she wants her table back bitch!" This classic case of your friend who is not my friend should not know our business-type situation.

Chapter Three

Feeling Ghosted

Once I finally decided to leave Andre alone, I was only seeing or focusing on Scrappy. We have spent a lot of time together; he stayed the night at my house quite often. He told me he felt at peace when he was lying in my bed. No stress and no worries. I was beginning to have strong feelings for him. I asked him if he felt that way too. All he could say was he felt something and he didn't know what else to say. Right then and there I should have just let it be. At times I wish I was made different. Without an open heart, without caring so much about other people. Not being so trusting or just not being so naive. I was in desperate need of attention from a man all the time because that made me feel beautiful. No one wants to ever confess to that, I had to face the fact that at forty-five years old, I was still dealing with low self-esteem issues. Two months after we just hanging out and chilling, I started seeing a change in him. He wasn't calling me as often or when I called him he didn't answer the phone. I kind of felt like he was pulling away from me. So instead of me being a grown woman and just walking away, what did I do? I chased him. And that is never a good thing to do. Two weeks went by, no call, no show, no nothing. I kind of gave up at that point. So I started to talk to one of the ambulance drivers at my job. This guy is named Omar. He was so fine and he made me laugh. The problem with him was he was married. I didn't ever want to sleep with a married man. He was from Jamaica he treated me kindly. He was always respectful. He bought me lunch a few times I never thought about having an affair with him. Omar had given me his number a long time ago. I never used it because he was married. However now that I'm feeling some sort of way about Scrappy ghosting me, it was time to see what else was out there. I was so deep in my feelings I felt I needed someone's shoulder to cry on. When I saw Omar at work, something came over me. He looked at me and asked if everything was okay. At that moment I felt a tear drop from my eye. Omar immediately grabbed me put his arms around me and said everything is going to be okay, I'm here for you. I asked him if he wanted to come back to my place when he got off of work. I just wanted to talk. He said he would be by after he finished his shift. I gave him my address. He was due to get off at ten o'clock that morning. He knocked on the door at about eleven a.m. I opened the door this man was so fine. Them juicy lips were calling my name. They looked so delicious I wanted to snatch him up so bad! Whew, just let me breathe, let me breathe, let me breathe, he walked in and all I could do was picture him with his shirt off and those grey sweatpants with that extremely long, fat bulge in the front definitely was not keeping me cool either. Yasssss hunty, don't get me started on that accent either. That accent did it for me every time. He walked in and started tonguing me down like I was his lost Lover from way back when. A scene straight out of a romantic movie. I shouted out with despair... wait, wait, wait! I didn't want this. Excuse me, but you're married! He apologized. Please forgive me for misunderstanding your invitation. If he could read my thoughts on that moment, that was exactly what I wanted. My initial intention for inviting him over was to just basically get some things off my chest and I wanted to hear a man's perspective of what was happening between Scrappy and me. But after seeing him and I have no self control I don't like the fact that I was desperate at that time I wanted to get my mind off of Scrappy. Just as the saying goes," A way to get over a man is to get under a new man!" At the time I was deeply hurt and wanted that pain to go away. I didn't care about his wife at that time. To be honest, I just wanted my needs met and he was a willing participant.

We sat on the couch in my living room. I began to tell him what was going on with me. He said it sounded like Scrappy was playing the field he didn't want to be committed. He wanted the benefits of a relationship but he didn't want the actual commitment. So if you're cool with just having sex with him, let it be just that. Have sex with him don't get your feelings involved. Well, it was way too late for that. It must have been him ignoring my calls that did it. I felt neglected and unworthy. I had to remind myself that this was just a fling and technically he didn't owe me anything. A little respect would have been nice but everyone doesn't move like we would hope. Or they aren't mature enough to do right by people. Nevertheless, it hurt my feelings. Scrappy was the only one I was seeing at the time so it felt right in my mind and in my heart but way back in my mind, I knew that everything Omar just said to me was true I had to go with the flow we can be friends but keep it at distance I just felt so heartbroken. I was in a vulnerable state. Low enough, for Omar to slide right on in.

Ten minutes later, somehow we ended up in my bedroom. He wanted to take a shower real quick. So I gave him a towel. He came out I couldn't help but notice the little beads of water all down his body. I didn't know if I was lonely or just a plain old freak. Or maybe a little bit of both. I could not wait for him to take full advantage of me. He started kissing me, threw me on the bed and devoured my box. Lord, now I have had some good head in my time. He was right up there with that white guy named Larry. Larry can eat some pussy. He was a pleaser sexually. And he loved TF outta of black girls.

Omar, I think gave Larry your run for his money that day. Omar was definitely Mr. Loverman. He had me begging for help and climbing the walls. I didn't want him to stop. His phone rang, it was his wife. She wanted him to grab a few things from the store on his way home. He had to go. I definitely wanted his sex again and again! That was some powerful extraordinary sex! He went to wash up and got dressed. I walked him outside. We kissed each other and he drove off into the sunset. I looked down the street and it looked like Scrappy was going into Jennifer's house. I thought to myself did he see Omar leave my house? Why am I nervous about that? I haven't heard from this dude in 2 weeks. Nor are we in a relationship. This put me right back in my feelings about Scrap.

The sex with Omar was great but the connection to Scrappy was greater. It was only a temporary fix.

Now I'm back to focusing on Scrapp again, so I call him. This time Rah answers his phone. She told me he was sleeping so I politely said to her oh can you wake him up? She told me no I'll let him know that you called so we hung up and then I texted him...if you don't want to talk to me that's all you got to say I don't know why you let that girl answer your phone that's none of my business but that's not cool. I don't know if he showed her my text or if she read it on her own since she claimed he was asleep but later on, that night as I'm riding down the street on my way to work she sees me riding by so she starts yelling to me " I'm his sister Bitch!" She's not his blood sister but hood sister.

Remember I told you all this chick is crazy. Every little thing sets her off I didn't know dealing with this dude meant that I would have to deal with everybody that's in his presence. He's only 6 years younger than me but still is over the age of 18 and if he considers himself to be an adult everybody does not have the right to be in your business. This is some childish bullshit if you ask me. If I was fully aware of who I was at the time and I didn't let people play with me. I really felt that I would have never called him again. Since he didn't want to deal with me he got Rah to come after me. Scrappy and I were Facebook friends So later on after that incident he posted that he only has love for his sisters. His sisters Raniequa and Jennifer. He doesn't have time to love anybody else. This hood nigga who is grown by age but a child by his actions, was messy as hell. I felt like I was back in middle school with the nonsense he was putting me through. At that moment, I couldn't figure out why he turned on me just like that. The only thing that I could think was he must've been seeing somebody else or he had seen Omar come out of my house. Either way what's wrong with having a conversation about it and being polite?

Why all the unnecessary drama and chaos? I was really upset about that, but nobody would know that because I will always keep stuff to myself. I did confide in another Co-worker Mia. Who I thought was my friend too but apparently everybody that Iconsidered to be my friend either stabbed me in the back or walked away from me. I had to keep asking God why people keep leaving my life. I didn't know until I was older that God was protecting me from people that didn't belong in my life.

Chapter Four

Second Time Around

In October 2016 my lease was up on the house that I had on Chaplin Street. I didn't want to renew it. I had no clue where I was moving to next. I just knew I couldn't stay there any longer. The neighborhood was too violent. There was a shooting almost every day on the street behind me. Besides I had fallen out with Scrappy and Jennifer I just felt unwanted around there, I had to get away from there ASAP. I ended up moving with my sister she lived two blocks over from where we stayed on Chaplin. I took all my stuff and put it in storage. My daughter ended up going to stay with her father so she could continue to go to the school in Hamilton. The school district she went to was in a better neighborhood. So I preferred her to go to school there. So my son and I moved in with my sister Michelle and her three kids. Michelle is the baby of the family. My other sister Aisha was God knows where at that time. Aisha was no stranger to the hood because she was out there in the streets. She knew Scrappy before I did. In fact, she knew him very well. Aisha used to date one of his cousins. So when she found out that I met him, she gave me a warning to watch out for him. Her exact words were, "he's a piece of shit". But me being the kind-hearted person that I am, I thought that everybody deserves a chance. You are innocent until proven guilty in my book. That there lies the problem with me, I Always want or trust people to have the same heart as me.

One day I was sitting on my Sister Michelle's porch, it was early morning around eight. I saw Scrappy's car ride by. He had a silver 1998 Cadillac Seville Sts and you couldn't tell him that he wasn't Pimp Daddy of the Year in that car. He was always laid back with one hand on the wheel, blasting his hip-hop music to the 5th power. You always knew it was him when he rode by. The difference this time was Jennifer was driving his car and he was laid back in the passenger seat. I thought that was crazy but at the same time, I knew they were good friends. Maybe he wasn't feeling good that day but he still had to get his son to school. His son's school was around the corner from where I was staying. That was the first time that I saw them together. The next time that I saw them in the car together he was dropping her off to work. For whatever reason she no longer had a car. This time she made a point to talk to me. Even though we hadn't spoken in months she began to tell me that Scrappy wasn't just acting funny towards me he was acting funny towards the other girl he was messing with. I didn't know there was another girl but I suspected as much. He was giving Jennifer a ride to and from work because she was without a car at that time. Jennifer made a point to tell me that Scrappy picks her up from work in the morning, then they take his daughter and her son to work and then he goes to work. I was like wow, y'all just one big happy family over there huh? I was trying not to show my disgust, resentment or any other type of emotion towards her. I just thought to myself these people are all fucked up they are so shady and I'm glad I got from around there. After that conversation with Jennifer, I thought something was going on between those two but she was swearing up and down that it was nothing. Scrappy was her brother and she still was messing with his brother. I just let it be. I really didn't want to have anything to do with her anymore at this point. I continued to keep my distance from her.

A month has passed since I moved in with my sister. I continued my search to find a place of my own. My coworker Mia who I once considered a good friend also, told me about an extra room at the house where she was staying with her son's family. Basically her baby daddy's other son and the son's girlfriend Monica. I talked to Monica and she agreed to rent the room to me. I really needed to get out of my sister's house it wasn't working out. Plus this place was further away from Scrappy and his drama. Monica's man was locked up at the time so she said she could use the money. She had two small children, so the money would come in handy.

After I moved there I began to have car trouble. I was able to trade that clunker in for a more reliable car. Things were beginning to get better. So I thought. There was another girl that lived there as well. Now you have 4 grown Women, my 26-year-old son, three children under the age of ten and an annoying cat living in a three-bedroom house. A bit full if you ask me. I was at work one night when I got a call from Mia saying that Monica was arguing with her boyfriend's mom and other family members. The mom and the other family members came to the house and started taking stuff out of the house. They took a few pans that I had in the kitchen. The reason why they did that was because they found out Monica spent her boyfriend's money that he saved up before he got incarcerated. So they felt entitled to come take whatever they wanted out of the house. I was feeling some sort of way about that, so I went to get a hotel room that was across the street from the job. I stayed there for about 3 days just trying to figure out my next move. So while I was there I decided to give Scrappy a call. I was surprised that he answered. He told me his car was acting up. I agreed to go pick him up and bring him back to my room. When I got to his house he told me he needed a part for his car and asked me to take him to the auto store. Once we got to the auto store, he told me he needed an additional $20 for the part he was trying to get. I was really reluctant to give it to him because I don't like to give men money for anything, especially after what happened with Andre. But I gave it to him. Now we go to the hotel room. After we got reacquainted and took care of business, his phone rang. Someone had called him through Facebook Messenger. I saw the picture on his phone it was of a female named Veronica he immediately clicked it off.

Then he asked me to take him back home because he had to do something by six o'clock that evening. I ended up paying for an additional day at the room. Scrappy said that he could come back later when he got done doing what he had to do. So when later came around he was back to not answering my call. I called him the next day he still was ignoring me, so I left him a message that said "I knew that you had no intentions of coming back here I didn't think that you would not respond to me once again and I'm going to need my $20 back. No response. The next day he posts on his Facebook page that he's in a relationship with Veronica. Hold up wait one damn minute what is going on here? if you're in a relationship with someone that means you had to been talking and dealing with this chick before I picked you up the other day. You had me pick you up, have sex with you and you took my money? And now you don't want to give it back to me? and now you're talking about you're in a relationship? I was beyond in my feelings at this point. So since he wanted to play games with me I reported his Facebook page as being inappropriate and it got taken down and that was the last time I talked to him. I also sent Veronica a message as well. I said I lent your boyfriend some money and I would like it back he thinks he can just play games with people I'm not one of the people. She never responded to me but she told him about it of course. I hit my sister Aisha up and told her to reach out to him since she knew him. He tells her I gave him that money as a gift and that he told me he had a girlfriend. I said he was the biggest liar on the planet I was too old for this nonsense I was done at that time I didn't know what else to say. Honestly, how many more times does this man have to show me that he's a piece of shit before I get the message? Apparently, I didn't learn my lesson at all because that was not the end of him and not by a long shot.

Chapter Five

Third Times A Charm

It has always been said that everything happens for a reason. A lot of times we are put in places where you may meet people by accident but it was no accident. Alot of times we are assigned to people. They turn out to a blessing or a lesson. I am a firm believer in the word of God. However, I am not the most religious person when it comes to reciting the scripture. I consider myself to be very spiritual. I believe in things that are beyond our control.

That brings us to February 2017 Monica got word that her boyfriend was getting released from jail. So she panicked because the money that he had saved and left with her she spent it all. So she got scared and wanted to leave town. She wanted to take her two kids and move out of the state. But she neglected to tell me that. Mia told me the day before Monica was due to leave.

That meant I needed to find another place to live because remember I was only renting a room from her. She was actually renting the house through a friend of her family. So basically the landlord didn't know I was staying there. The day that Monica was due to leave I asked her for the landlord's number she gave it to me and I got in touch with the landlord and she agreed to rent out the house to me.

I always felt like this house fell right into my lap because I've been struggling for some time now and it started to feel like I was home. I prayed, prayed and prayed some more for me to find a stable home. That's why I always say the power of prayer is so powerful. You must pray and thank God daily. He makes all things possible. That's what I have always believed in ever since I was a little girl. I've always felt that way but didn't always walk in it. As I'm getting older I can see that it's more important to do so. Monica left that day, the other woman that was staying there was due to leave in a few days. Mia ended up quitting her job at the hospital and moving back to St Louis with her mother. So that left me and my son in the house. Now I wanted to get my daughter back with us but I also wanted her to finish school where she was at. So it was a little while before she came to join us at the house. Months started going by and now I'm looking at the house, a lot of work needs to be done. Plus I still had a whole house in storage. I didn't know how I was going to get everything to this new house. So I just had to wait for an opportunity because I didn't know too many people. I didn't know anybody around there, but life goes on. I continued to work and try to stay on top of everything. One day I looked on Facebook and I saw that Scrappy started a new Facebook page. He had a picture up there of him sitting at the bar.

He looked sad and depressed. According to his Facebook status, he said he was at the local bar getting a few drinks. People are doing the most on those Facebook statuses. They show where they're at, what they're eating and what they're doing at the time. I thought about going down there to talk to him. And at that moment I said no sit your ass down somewhere! Why do you keep thinking about this guy? This is crazy. And for the longest time after that moment, he was on my mind so bad. I felt it in my spirit and deep in my soul. He was hindering my spirit so badly. It was to the point where I could not shake it. I knew this dude was no good so why can't I get him out of my system? This went on for a couple of weeks and I said something to my friend Michael. He suggested that I get in touch with Scrappy because it was driving me crazy. I agreed. I was so nervous about calling him I have never felt this way about anybody. Especially somebody that moved like a snake in the grass. You would run for the hills not towards them. I called him I was surprised that he still had the same number. We talked and I invited him over.

It's becoming clear at this point. No matter how many times we fall off, we always come back together. We had sex. And right after sex, he said he wanted to tell me something. But first He wanted to know if I was the one that reported his page. I laughed and said yes that was me. He said I knew it was you! We talked about that and he told me he was no longer with Veronica, it just wasn't working out. However, they were still friends also he's still friends with all his exes. That should have been a red flag for me. I even thought to myself wow what's up with that? How is that possible I mean there were no ill feelings. Why aren't y'all still together? Y'all just figured that y'all weren't right for each other but decided to remain friends? Even though I had many questions, It still didn't bother me at that moment. We were having a deep conversation and I thought he was being honest and transparent. Then he had to look away from me, he couldn't look me in my eyes. He finally got up the courage to look at me and said I really got to tell you this. I was a little nervous at first. I had no clue as to what he needed to tell me. Then he just blurted out "I had sex with Jennifer!". Now any normal person in their right state of mind would have thrown his ass out. All I said was wow! I was not expecting that, it blew my mind for a moment. Then I asked, was it during the time that you were seeing me? He said no but it was after I had moved off of the street. I kind of figured something was going on because her face was lighting up when she was telling me about you. it was like she was in love or something. He said yes she had got infatuated and was catching feelings so he had to cut it off. I said pretty much like you did when we first started messing around. I was catching a feeling so you figured you had to cut me loose. He laughed and said, "I plead the fifth". I'm going to laugh with you because right now we just having sex. I don't want anything from you. That day he left a week later he came back and we've been talking the whole week getting along great and I was like okay he's cool we're back to being cool again. He called me one night and asked me to give him a ride in the morning to his coworker's house so he could catch a ride to work with him. I didn't realize at the time that this was going to be a daily trip. I basically agreed to it because I was starting to like him and I thought we were friends. I just thought I was helping my friend out but here I go back in my feelings again. Now the connection is getting stronger and stronger and he starts telling me he's happy and he feels good about himself. I was happy too at that time. One night on November 18th 2017, I asked him "Are we a couple now"? That sounds so lame saying it out loud. He hesitated for a moment and said yes. A week prior to that he said he wasn't ready to be in a relationship. However, once I asked him if he wanted to relationship with me he agreed to be in a relationship with me. He said yes! I can admit that that's how it happened initially he did say he did not want a relationship but then agreed to be in one with me, let's keep that in mind. We did what we do best, fucking like porn stars. He went to take a shower. He left his phone on the charger. Someone began blowing his phone up. Even though we just became a couple 5 minutes ago I was going to let him tell whoever was calling his phone to stop calling his phone. But my nosey ass goes and looks at the phone. I see this picture of this woman's ass as a screensaver for the person who was calling. I remember the name, the name was saved as Nelly.

So now that we're a couple things really started to take off. I ignored the fact that females were still calling his phone. Although he would not answer in my presence I knew he was still talking to some of them at first I couldn't decipher who he was messing with or who was just his family or who he considered family. Scrappy had so much family all around town.

I often wondered how this man took my soul. Then I remembered how he used to sing and rap to me. He used to throw it on thick. Although most of his rhymes were wack, I enjoyed his flow.

When he sang to me, he would look deep into my eyes. The passion was mesmerizing. He definitely had me feeling myself.

I remember saying to him that I would like his help with the house. I'm new to being in a house this large. So I'm going to need a little bit of help. He agreed to help me with everything. Months go by we spend Thanksgiving, Christmas, his mom's birthday and my birthday together...Everything was going great. At the beginning of January 2018, he stayed at my house for three nights in a row. Since his car was in the shop once again, I took him back home. Once we pulled up on his street, we saw fire trucks, an ambulance and police cars. We had no clue as to what was going on. As we get closer to his mother's house, the house is on fire. His 11-year-old son started the fire in the house. It was unclear where the fire started. They just knew it was upstairs. So immediately they grabbed what they could out of the house put it in my car and I told them they could stay with me until they figured it out. This is how he and his son came to live with me. I can see the hurt and shame all over DaShawns face. Dashawn said he didn't mean to start the fire. He was burning a candle and went to the kitchen to get a snack. He didn't realize the candle had fallen over. That was the story he gave us at first. Scrappy was a different person at that time he was so angry with his son. Naturally, he was very emotional. The house they lived in for so long was burnt to the ground. He made a post on Facebook expressing how disappointed he was with his son and can't wait to send him back to his mom. I told him to take it down. You can't say that about your child online it's not fair to your child you can't do that. A few days after being in my house, DaShawn started being disrespectful to me. He had no respect for me, my house and especially not for his dad. I told him we're not going to do that I know you don't know me and we don't know each other but you're in my house now and you're going to have to respect that. We had a nice long conversation. A couple of weeks go by, now Dashawn and I see eye to eye. He's starting to listen to me he's starting to open up to me. He admitted to me that he set his dad's clothes on fire because his dad had not been there in days. He did not hear from his dad in days. I felt so bad at that time because I had no idea that this was going on with these two. Scrap had the world believing that he was the best dad in the world. Meanwhile, he didn't care anything about his son. He only cared about his son when it made him look good that's God's honest truth.

Chapter Six

Locked in

My daughter came to live with us in August of last year. So she was there when Scrappy and I became a couple. However, she didn't meet DaShawn, Scrappys son until the night of the fire. We ultimately became one big happy family. Despite all the ups and downs that occurred along the way. We all were getting along so we'll. I met a lot of his family. Like I said earlier he has family all across the city. I met most of them. Some of them have even been chilling at my house.

Even Ranieka and I made amends.

The first time that we celebrated his birthday together, was the night I fell in love with him. Prior to that, he made me feel alive again. He was so attentive to my every need. He cleaned out my basement even got a team together to get my stuff out of storage. They moved everything into my house. I thanked him and I thanked God for bringing us back together. We were in what you call the honeymoon phase. I was falling so deep real fast. I believe he knew he had me locked in. I was singing love songs again. Making posts on Facebook about how nice it is to love again.

I would blast some R&B love songs while cleaned the house. Everything was going great, until it wasn't. While I was cleaning the bathroom, Scrappy came in to give me a kiss and stated that he'll be back. He's going around the way for a bit. This was the start of him hanging out and leaving me in this relationship alone. On this particular night in April 2018, Scrappy didn't come home after hanging out with his cousins. I sat in the front room waiting for him to come in. It was six o'clock in the morning when he did come into the house. He acted as if he didn't see me sitting there. He walked right past me to the kitchen and put his phone on the charger. I asked, where have you been? And why was your phone off? Of course, he said my bad Bae, my phone died. I was passed out drunk at Tony's house. His phone rang. He acted like he didn't hear it. So I picked up his phone and answered it but they hung up. There was no picture or name stored for the person that was calling his phone. However, I do remember the number and it belonged to none other than Mz Nelly herself. So I questioned him as to why this lady would be calling him at six o'clock in the morning. He snatched his phone from me. Oh, I see... Is that where you were, with her? He began to get agitated and threw his phone. Then ran down to the basement. I picked up the phone, now I saw a text message between him and her he was telling her to meet him at his cousin Tony's house the night before and then there was no communication after that. So you were with her at your cousin's house is that what I'm reading? He got so upset and started screaming at me. Now we're going back and forth. This is 6 months into our relationship. Things got so heated and out of control, extremely fast. Then it happened, he slapped me across the face I fell onto the floor. He didn't mean to hit me he just lost control. I threatened to call the cops. So he ran out of the house I don't know where he went at that time. The kids were crying and screaming they couldn't believe what was going on. He came back in through the back door and was screaming at me, "Oh you're going to call the cops on me I'm going to lose my son" Because he did have custody of his son. Well you shouldn't have put your hands on me, you're the one in all the way wrong here! Why did I not kick him out of the house at that moment? I guess me being the good person that I am once again. I felt bad because they had nowhere else to go. I left the house.

I'm in such disbelief but guess what? Me being a mother and a strong Woman... I still had to take the kids to school. The kids went to two different schools neither one was close to the other in fact in completely opposite directions. I remember DaShawn and I were in the car the song “When We” by Tank came on and I lost it. That was one of the songs that Scrappy and would make love to, it was so inappropriate to be listening to with a minor child in the car. After I broke down in tears, I quickly turned it off. DaShawn asked me why I cried so hard when that song came on. Little boy, mind your business.

Is that the third or fourth red flag? I lost count. Let's recap…

Community service

Lives with mom

Temporary employment

Multiple exes or females within a year

Neglected his minor child

Loses control easy/ put hands on me

excessive use of drugs and alcohol

OH Wait, we haven't even discussed number seven yet. My bad y'all.That evening once we all got settled in for the night, Scrappy came in about seven p.m. He was high as shit. He sat on the bed next to me looking sad and pitiful. Declaring his love and appreciation for me and begging me to give him another chance. I was already in way too deep with my feelings. Knowing that all of what happened should have never happened. But because I was weak for this man, I agreed to give him another chance. Little did I know that this was going to be the beginning of an ongoing roller coaster ride that I would be begging to get off.

A few weeks go by, I get a call from my sister Michelle. She tells me she has something very important to tell me. One of her good friends knows another female who knows Scrappy and according to that female Scrappy is still involved with his ex Nelly and she knows that because she has seen them together multiple times since we've been in a relationship. Scrappy was at work when I got this call so I called him up and I questioned him about what I had just heard. Of course, he denied it then he proceeded to call my sister to cuss her out and called her outside of her name. I had to go to work early that night so I wasn't at the house when he came home.

When I came home in the morning he was not there he had taken his son to stay with the baby mama. He calls and tells me he'll be by to get the rest of his stuff he's staying at Rah's house. I said why is that? He said I told you I'm not messing around with nobody and you don't believe me. So I felt like I shouldn't be there and he hung up on me. Now I'm going crazy trying to get him back on the phone because at this moment it's like somebody ripped my heart out of my chest and I didn't know how to handle it. So instead of me letting him go at that moment I begged him to come back. We argued for the rest of the day on the phone. A couple of days went by I didn't hear from him I told him I was going to take the rest of his stuff and put it on his mom's porch since he didn't want to be there. He had a problem with that. He proceeds to ask me if he could leave his stuff there till he finds another place and he feels bad about what happened he feels like a bum on the street because he had to go stay with his home girl. I said well you should have thought about that before things spiraled out of control.

I agreed to him leaving his stuff at my house. Also, I told him he could stay although he made it clear on Facebook that he was single again. Now DaShawn was staying with the baby's mom Lakeisha. I have never talked to or met her in person. Lakeisha had to go to work one day, so she tried to drop DaShawn off at my house, unannounced while Scrappy was still at work. I told her that I was not a babysitter. Scrappy and I broke up and it was not my job to watch the boy. That's not my problem if you have to work to find a sitter. Lord, why did I become public enemy number one behind this foolishness? Scrappy had the whole hood including his momma telling him I was wrong for that! First off the baby mom was rude as hell to me. She began calling me Spongebob because to her I had no shape. She also said that she hoped that her baby daddy would find someone better-looking. So at that point, I blocked her from my phone. Why on earth would I allow you to disrespect me and leave your son with me until his dad got home? This man did all he could to make me look foolish. Why would I allow that? Scrappy was pissed that I said she couldn't drop his son off to me. He felt wherever he laid his head, his son should be welcomed. That's a true statement. However, no one discussed with me what they wanted to do. Let's not forget how he cheated, lied and tried to manipulate the situation making everything my fault. These people had no respect, no boundaries, no morals whatsoever I put my foot down that day. I should have left it down and been done with the whole situation. I guess I'm just a glutton for punishment.

Once again I talked him into staying with me. I know what you all are thinking, when is this madness going to end? I was thinking the same thing too. What is wrong with me? Why can't I just let this man go? Clearly, he does not want me, he does not want to be here. For some reason, I just can't let him be. I keep inserting myself into his life. Now I have to ask the question to God. What is going on with me? Honestly, God told me there's still work to be done. I always believed that God bought us together for a reason. God put me in his life to help him get himself together and to stop all the foolishness that he was doing. Also for me to do the same thing. I always felt that God put him in my life to help me get my finances in order. For me to stop gambling. When we became a couple I immediately stopped going to the casino. I wanted this relationship to work. I wanted us to be together. I wanted a future with him. What God didn't tell me was nothing about this situation was going to be easy. I had no idea what I was up against or how I would survive.

Chapter Seven

Lessons And More Lessons

Once he came back to my house, things were still rocky. It seems like every day there was a new challenge. He left his son with the baby's mom, Lakeisha. They went to court to try to see if Lakeisha could have custody of their son. Unfortunately, they could not give her custody because she had another Dfys case open. She could only get supervised visits. Lakeisha brought Dashawn back to my house. He immediately ran to me and hugged me and said they were telling them that he was not allowed to be with his mom. He really wanted to live with her. I felt so bad for him. In my opinion neither one of his parents was capable of taking care of him. Not only did they not have a stable home, they did not have a safe environment. From what I heard about the baby's mom, she had a lot going on in her personal life. And is super ghetto. The dad is never around for the boy, but this is the person that I chose to be with. I thought maybe with my help he would have a better relationship with his son. All we can do is hope and dream. But if it's not in him to do so, it's not in him to do so.

The caseworker showed up at my house. She had to investigate the premises. She walked through the entire house to make sure it was a suitable place for Dashawn to stay. Now I'm involved in this Boy's Life whether or not Lakeisha wanted me to be.

Scrappy listed me as Dashawns emergency contact at school and everywhere else that he went to. I was the emergency contact. So now I'm the Stepmom without being married.

I was all for it because I was beginning to have a real genuine bond with DaShawn.You know he had my heart.

Things were starting to feel normal again. Basically, everywhere I went DaShawn went. I showed him how to wash his clothes he helped me around the house he went to the grocery store with me I bought the things he needed. He was my third child no doubt. He has helped me a lot and I helped him a lot. Basically, whatever he needed I provided for him.

Scrappy's car got repoed. So now we had to figure out how he was to get back and forth to work. The time that he needed to go to his coworker's house for a ride would have interfered with the kids getting to school. No worries Superwoman to the rescue. His job was forty-five minutes away from where we lived. My routine for the next year and a half was:Come home from work Take a 15-minute nap Go drop Stacey off, Go drop Scrappy off, Go drop Dashawn off

Then go home and go to sleep provided I had nowhere to go that morning or afternoon. now because I'm on a set schedule I had a routine before these people came to live with me I would cook dinner at a certain time and lay back down and take a nap before my shift at work. Now I have all these extra responsibilities and Duties. if I wanted to make dinner that night dinner has been cooked and finished by two o'clock p.m. Because now everybody I dropped off in the morning I got to go back and pick them all back up this was my life for a year and a half. While I chose to do all of that for everyone in the house, I neglected myself. I wore myself completely out and I take full responsibility for that. I did not have to take that grown man who is not my husband to work. Nor did I have to take a child who is not my child and has two parents to school. For a while, I didn't mind because this was my family now. In mist all that, Scrappy began to hang out every night once again. Not only was this relationship a roller-coaster ride it was probably one of the biggest lessons that I had to endure in my entire life.

I noticed he was becoming distant towards me again. He seemed depressed a lot. I thought it was because he didn't have his own place, plus he was broke all the time. I understood and was willing to help him in any way that I could. But he was good at shutting me out. Or just not being there for me at all. I got no attention. I remember saying I wished he would just focus on me for a change.

At this point, we haven't had sex In a long time. He told me that he believes he has a problem getting it up. And wanted to seek help. I believed him and looked for a doctor who specializes in that area. Well, he almost had me yet again. More lies... According to the females that he had conversations with on his phone, suggested otherwise. It appears that he's having sex just not with me. Here I am all in for this dude. Going out of my way.

Catering to his every need. Taking care of his son. Paying all the bills in my house. He spends zero time with me but entertains everybody in the hood. I can't even get a back rub from him or even a thank you. At this point, it's time to wrap this shit up. I'm mad angry hurt confused and disgusted. I was quiet about what I saw on his phone this time. He asked me to drop him off in town one night. As we were riding in the car Queen Naija's new song "Medicine" came on…

Why is she singing about my life right now? I swear that was exactly what we have been going through. This is insane, how things show up for me. This was a trend that I experienced. Things always fell right in my lap. I looked at him and said this relationship is not working for me. He looked away from me. I dropped him off at his designation. And didn't see him again until I came home from work the next morning. He informed me he wanted to leave. Then starts yelling at me for going in his phone again. Basically tells me it's my fault because I work every weekend. And that's the only time he can spend with me. So everything is my fault. Is it my fault that you can't keep your penis in your pants? Is it my fault that you talk to other females on the phone, online and outside? Is it my fault that you can't live your best life? Is it my fault that you don't have a car? Is it my fault that you can't take care of your son? Meanwhile, I'm running around here doing everything I can to make sure he and his son are taken care of. I even allowed him to use my car. I allowed him to do whatever he basically wanted because I didn't want to upset him. We always did what he wanted to do. Every time I would plan something for us to even with the kids, he was either hung over or too drunk. Again I had to ask God what exactly was wrong with me. I had to dig deep down in my soul to try to figure out what was going on here. Clearly, this man has no problem disrespecting me. I kept allowing this disrespect to continue. I kept allowing him to embarrass me. I kept allowing the foolishness. All I could do was sweep it under the rug and tell him that I was there for him because clearly he was hurting and I'm sorry that I caused him any pain. Jesus save me please I am so into this person so attached to this person that I am starting to normalize his bad behavior. I am starting to apologize for his bad behaviour I am normalizing his disrespect to the point where it doesn't even bother me anymore. After I cried about it two times and saw that he was a piece of shit. I accepted the fact that that's how he is that's who he is. But why do I still want him? What is wrong with me.? After all, what good does venting do if you don't do anything about it? I felt like I accepted his behaviour because I wasn't a perfect person either. I have watched this man act like a child, and shift blame on everything and everybody else. While he took no accountability for his actions. Nothing was ever his fault. I have watched him literally fight demons that I knew nothing about. I just feel so bad for him and I wanted to help him. But soon I had to realize I had my own things to battle. You can't fix everybody. Whatever he is battling is not my problem. It's not my fight to fight. He has to face whatever he is fighting within himself by himself.

After all, I was going through a grieving period and nobody was there to console me or to comfort me. I had to go through it by myself and just like I had made poor choices in my life nobody helped me fix those wrongs I had to work on it by myself I have some flaws although I did not cheat like he did I just felt like my credit was so bad I wanted to just get my life together I feel like at forty-something years old I have failed myself. So I had a lot of insecurities that's why I felt the way I did. My finances were a mess I didn't think I was pretty enough I didn't think anybody wanted me I was too shy to be around people I had a lot of insecurities so having this man by my side meant a lot to me I felt secure again I felt like I was the most beautiful person in the world. That's the way he made me feel. I felt like we belonged together. So once I became attached to him it was hard to detach myself. I was not strong at all. I was not as strong as I thought I was. I can admit I was a mess. I guess I didn't want me alone. To me, my future was pretty dark without a person there beside me. I know that you have to find happiness within yourself not in another person. Even though I know that I couldn't help the way I felt. My insecurities were so strong that I allowed this man to walk me like a dog. I allowed him to mistreat me. Then try to turn it around on me I felt bad. So apologizing to him was all I could do. He helped me spend my money. Just about every time we went out, I footed the bill. For every cookout we had, I paid for everything. He didn't spend anything on me. If he did it was a rare occasion. I got fed up one day and asked him "Why exactly are you here with me if you are not helping me do anything?" you're just leeching off of me. Getting what you can out of me. You have a built-in babysitter for your son. You still want to hang out in the streets you don't want to be here, or spend time with him or me. Why are you here? Please let me know. His response to that was he didn't know. I don't know how many more months after this he stayed. Officially we broke up a total of three times. These little ins and outs here and there didn't count as a breakup I guess after this incident we were back to talking again everything was fine. Now I'm feeling like he's not my man, but some sort of project. As in I'm doing a case study on him. Basically, he won't leave my house I feel like his son still needs me since the Mother wasn't allowed to have him at the time so I'm still here for his son. His son and I got so close. His son was telling me things that his dad was doing outside of the house far as looking at women walking down the street, and hollering at them. Great now you're showing your son this bad behavior! Hollering out the car window... hey girl how are you doing, you looking good, you look beautiful. He was still hanging out every night. One time my sister Michelle said she saw him sitting on the steps and he just looked so sad and depressed like he didn't have a friend in the world I said yeah he's mad at me because he doesn't have a car, he doesn't have a place to live. He's broke all the time and he has to face the fact that he got his son with him. Whatever the case might have been he didn't feel like he needed me even though I was there. I came to terms with that like you cannot fix a grown man at all. You cannot tell him to act like a grown man he has to do that on his own.

Chapter Eight

It's All My Fault

One night Scrappy and I were lying in bed and he was showing me something on his Facebook page. He clicked on the search bar I saw in the search bar the name of one of his ex-girlfriends. So I asked him. why he was searching for Veronica up? He tried to tell me that it was old. That it has been there for a while, he never erased it. However, my intuition would suggest otherwise. I let it go at that moment. I didn't say anything else about it. Just know my spidey senses were tingling. Time to put on my inspector gadget hat. Now this would be the start of me looking through his phone on a regular. I never wanted to look through his phone because if I need to look through your phone we don't need to be together. Prior to that, I started seeing a change in his behaviour. He started drinking more, he needed a bottle of Hennessey every day along with his beer and weed. He already was popping perks. Scrappy was always looking for some e-pills. He was obsessed with them. Although I didn't agree with them, the sex was phenomenal when he took them. It's not often that you find someone as freaky as you, he was definitely my match.

Back to looking at his phone. I waited until he was passed out drunk. I had to use his finger to unlock his phone. Man Oh Man talk about opening Pandora's Box. I don't think y'all are ready for what I discovered in this phone. It still gives me chills to this day. Since this man did not have a car I allowed him to use my car to go hang out with his Peeps. That was probably one of my biggest mistakes. Since I worked at night that gave him the perfect opportunity to cheat.

Remember I said you are innocent until proven guilty. Now one would argue I had no business going in that phone but on the other hand, what I discovered in that phone would have been the perfect recipe for an episode of how to get away with murder. I searched up and down and all around in that phone Not only was this man messing with one of his exes but two of his exes then flirting with multiple females on Messenger. Multiple text messages to different girls. When I told you my heart completely dropped to the floor, that phone was so hot it could have self-destructed in my hands. There was a video in there of him fucking one of them from the back. I don't know if the video was new or if it was old at that moment. I should have woken him up and kicked him out of my house. But no I sat on it for a couple of days trying to collect myself trying to figure out my next move. When he woke up for work the next morning I told him I was not taking him to work I was tired he would have to get there the best way he could. Of course, he got angry. So he didn't go to work that day he asked me if he could use the car after I dropped the kids off at school I told him no. He got so angry, asking me if I wanted him to lose his job. I said first of all, why are you back being friends with your ex Veronica on Facebook? He said oh, that's what this is about? You're mad because of social media? That's just social media, he explained. This man got so mad I said what are you mad for? Oh because I wouldn't let you use the car? This dude really tried to spin this on. Had the nerve to ask me 'How would it feel if my girlfriend wouldn't let me use the car to go to work?' First of all, it is not my responsibility to get you to and from work. I was doing that out of the kindness of my heart, but now since you want to mess with every bitch on the fucking planet. You get there the best way you can. His response was "I ain't messing with nobody!" I said oh so all these females in your phone all this nakedness that's going on in your phone you ain't messing with nobody? Oh, you went through my phone? He shouted, I hate this shit!

I have never in my life seen a man act more like a child than a grown man. Who is this person who I have sought after to be my man? The only real tears I saw this man shed was when his mom's house burned down. Any tears after that were pure manipulation. They were not real. It was so he could get whatever he wanted. Whenever I told him no he couldn't have something or he couldn't do something he turned into this six-year-old boy. The first time I saw that it was heartbreaking I was shocked I suppose this is when I started to feel more like his mother than his girlfriend he even told me one time I was acting like his mom because I needed him to pay some bills and or do the yard work. He felt like I was talking to him like he was my child. Well, you were acting like you were my child. And what do mothers do? They give you unconditional love. He was getting all of my unconditional love. I gave this man everything when he deserved nothing.

After all the discoveries that I found on his phone, I still did not kick him out of my house and out of my life. He left that day once again and returned home at night apologizing. There was no apology good enough on this Earth for you to say to me at this moment. He said he was willing to go to counseling to get help because at this point I'm looking at him like he's a sex addict and he tells me it's the pills and the alcohol. No, you do those things because you chose to do those things and I am sitting here willing to help you because I choose to help you yes this is crazy this is absolutely crazy this man had no regard for my health my safety or well-being hell I didn't even know at the time that I was so broken that I didn't even have any of those things for myself so I continue to stay with him I continue to give him love I continue to pour into him he gave me the bare minimum he did the bare minimum and I just sat there and allowed this to go on. This was the first year that we lived together. 2018 my birthday we went to Atlantic City with his job. It was a good time. After we got back that weekend he didn't go to work for 3 days he ended up getting fired. Now I'm really looking at him differently because you have no regard for your job every time you missed work was because you were hungover and then when I couldn't get you to work that one day you made it my fault that you were going to lose your job I don't understand how I allowed this person to treat me the way he did and I did absolutely nothing about it. We stayed together for more years after that. Over the years he did get a little better but that didn't stop him from cheating that didn't stop me from looking at his phone that didn't stop me from calling a female. That didn't make me throw him out we went on about our daily business we had arguments here and there I think he broke up with me a total of three times during the course of the 5 years and each time I allowed him to come back.

So let's get back to the ex-Veronica. He swore up and down he wasn't messing with her I let it go at the time a couple of weeks later before he went to work he gave me the best sex, even went down on me. He called that "giving me a treat" We haven't had sex in a couple of months. He even got up and made me breakfast that morning before he went to work I felt so special and so loved I was starting to feel good about us again. He came home from work and couldn't wait to hit the streets again. The reason why he felt so happy I thought it was because of me. No, he was fucking Veronica again. Now I'm looking at him as a case study because clearly, something is seriously wrong here now I can see one of the tell-tell signs when he's cheating. His behaviour tells on him every single time. He needs multiple women to mess with. Multiple women to make him feel good about himself. And every time he gets a little bit of money he feels like he's on top of the world. When he doesn't have any money you become his enemy. He treats you like you're his enemy. Upon going through his phone yet again. I see that maybe he's looking for somebody who he can manipulate. He's telling these females behind my back that it's not working out between us. Basically, I'm not doing this, I'm not doing that. When in fact I'm doing everything. I'm the only one in this relationship. Not to mention, I'm still taking care of his son.

So needless to say I could see everything that was going on everything that was wrong and I still didn't put a stop to it. So I'm going to take full accountability for the part that I played in hurting my own self hurting my own heart and allowing this person to walk me like a dog. Disrespect and embarrass me over and over again. Damn, I sound like a broken record. Part of the reason why I think that I stayed with him was because it was embarrassing as hell to tell anybody any of this. The little bit of time and effort that he gave me, I must've been satisfied with. I had to ask myself, what is wrong in my life to make you satisfied with the bare minimum? Something is clearly wrong. Honestly, after a while, the disrespect just felt normal. It was just like, oh well I didn't get upset about it. It didn't hurt me no more I was numb to the bullshit. I know it wasn't right.

Then the loneliness would kick in every now and then. At the same time, I was glad he was lying next to me at night. I was glad he was helping me the little bit that he did.

He still was hanging out but I knew where he was every night when he did hang out. Because now he's not allowed to answer his phone. We did get that straightened out but look how long it took us to get to that point. And now he's getting his finances together. His credit score is looking better. He's starting to be a little bit more respectful. I mean he already had it in him to be a good dude but when we got together it was like he wasn't done playing around he wasn't ready to be in a relationship financially spiritually emotionally. He just was not ready. I convinced myself that's what made me be okay with the bullshit. He simply was not ready. So all of that falls back on me. Again what is wrong with me for me to allow this person to manipulate me, to control me, to basically take my whole entire being over. What is wrong with me? For me dealing with him was starting to feel like a project. Like I was being paid to study him.

Eventually, I guess I got fed up and tired of all the nonsense. So it was time to have a serious talk with him. I told him I was not going to be around here catering to his every need. I do not tolerate it no more! I needed for him to leave. I said you could stay here until you find something else. I'll even help you get your shit together but I don't want to be with you no more because you are not here for me. I don't know what part of that conversation made him do a complete turnaround but I was thankful. It seems like after that day something clicked in his head. He was telling me he was done messing with those e-pills. He wasn't coming home pissy drunk like he used to. I felt like he was seeing the bigger picture now and that he wanted to be with me. So now we're actually living like a couple that is working towards a common goal to better ourselves. To better our relationship, show up for each other. Our connection was very strong, we mirrored one another. Now he's making plans with me. He's saying maybe WE can do THIS and do that. Everything was WE now, it was good. Scrappy was working with me instead of against me. I always knew he had this in him but the demonic forces were controlling his every move. Yes, I said demonic forces!

Chapter Nine

A Rude Awakening

2021 days before my 50th birthday Scrappy bought covid-19 into the house. He got it from one of his cousins. So now he's sick. As well as his son Dashawn, my daughter Stacy and me. We all got covid-19. I was actually diagnosed on the day of my 50th birthday.

They all had it worse than I did. The only symptom I showed initially was a fever. They all had a horrible cough, couldn't smell and couldn't taste anything. One thing that I did not like about this whole relationship was the fact that he couldn't keep his ass in the house. He always used to tell me he didn't like staying in the house. His life was one big party filled with no responsibility or no real direction. I wouldn't be so mad if he was out working instead of hanging out every night. This man is in his mid-40s. And refusing to grow up. One of his passions was to rap. Like I said I don't like his Rhymes but his flow is nice. He didn't have a rap status like the guys that are celebrating 50 Years of Hip Hop and surely did not fit in that category. Every time he would miss work he would still hang out that night. That bothered me a lot too. After a while, you get tired of having the same conversation. Especially with a person who is too old even to know better. What I was starting to realize was he may never change. Especially if I'm enabling his bad behaviour. I had to take full accountability for my part in the failed relationship or better yet this fucked up situationship.

Now some of the bills started piling up. He was barely helping me pay anything.

Whenever he did stay in the house he was on the internet researching different things about the Our culture, worldly remedies or conspiracy theories. A lot of things were enlightening. It did make me take a hard look at what we are putting in our bodies. I wouldn't say this relationship was a total loss after all he made me feel alive again in the beginning he made me feel like I had a sense of purpose once again. Although I truly feel like I did love him, it was the ongoing battle of trying to love him or for him to love me. It's true what they say, "You never know someone till you live with them". Let the person do what they want to do so you can see what they rather are doing. When a person shows you who they are the first time believe them. Or my old-time favourite, You can't raise a man! PERIOD!!

In May of 2022, Dashawn went to permanently live with his Mom Lakeisha. Although I would miss him terribly, I understood. Besides they both needed each other. I said to myself, I wonder how much longer Scrappy was going to stay with me after his son left. Even though Scrappy and I seemed like we had finally got a the same page.. In the back of my mind, I feared being abandoned again. And I always felt like he was using me to take care of his son.

Looking at Scrappy's life and everything he brought to my life, it wasn't a total loss. Something was keeping me here trying to love him. It was something that I could not even understand myself. What is this great force that is making me stay in the situation?

I see what's going on, I see who he is, who he truly really is. But yet I am still choosing to love him. Now I'm in deep deep Solitude with myself and trying to understand how to get out of the situation. Because it is not doing me any good nor am I helping him get better by allowing his behaviour. So then I started praying to God to remove me from this situation or to make it better. But once I have seen him going back to the way he used to be, not caring about anything or anybody. I couldn't take it anymore so I asked God please get me out of this situation I did not want to make a legal stand to remove him from my house. So I had to call on a higher power after all this time I grew tired I'm getting older my body is really starting to talk to me.

I start seeing a cardiologist. Started looking into how to better myself physically and mentally. I had to go through a series of tests. This was right around his birthday 2023 I allowed him to use my car to get back and forth from work and some days I had a doctor's appointment so he couldn't use my car. That meant he had to find a ride to work because after he got rid of his last car I told him I was not going to be able to take him to and from work. I am very tired and if you can't respect that, then there's something wrong with you. I have been here throughout the years for him and he should at least have some common decency to say okay babe I understand. And you being a man that you claim that you are should not depend on me as much as you do or have in the past. The day of his birthday he went to work that was the last time I spoke to him. He didn't come straight home after work. I just figured he went to go see his family members, okay I can give him that. But here he goes disrespecting me, once again. What's wrong with calling me and saying that you're going to do x y and z so the whole day I said I'm not even going to talk to him not going to contact him now I'm ready to go to work he's still not home yet. Right at that moment all I could think of was all the lying and cheating he has done throughout the years. All the tears, the arguments, the forgiveness and disrespect he has shown me.

Anything and everything that I did was for him. I gave this person so much grace and I gave myself none. This was the final straw. You claim to be my husband but you still treat me like I'm an option.

When he came into the house. I just lost it I said I'm done playing house with you. For now, you go do what you need to do, I'm going to do what I need to do. This is not the relationship that I want to be in. You have no respect for me and frankly, I'm tired of it. For the first time in a long time, it felt good to stand up for myself. In the back of my mind and in my heart I did not want him to go. But I know I was tired of being treated like this. I guess I felt like he should recognize his wrongdoings see my pain and try to fix this and himself. But in the end, he still didn't choose me. He decided that he wanted to leave.

However, he did not express that to me. He went behind my back and found his own place. In the days leading up to him moving out, he still played on me. He still played with me he did not tell me he was moving out. He continued to use my car to get to and from work. I found out because I went through his things and found a receipt for an apartment. So I said I'm not going to say anything about it I'm going to wait for him to tell me. He did not tell me then one Saturday I took off from work I said you know maybe we can go out and maybe try to salvage this relationship he left early that morning and did not return. He played around with me all day long about what time he was coming back home and never did. He decided to text me around nine p.m. that night saying that he found his own place and he was not coming back He'd be back tomorrow to get his things. I immediately took all of his things and gathered everything up together for him to pick up he's lucky I did not throw everything out on the street. The next day he came to get his things and had the audacity to ask me to help him take some things to his new place since he couldn't fit anything else in his brother's car. Hell NO! You left me. Obviously, he had a plan. Might have been planning this for a while. So you get your shit the best way that you can. I am done with you and this situation I never want to go back to it. As they say, Never Say Never.

The day he left, I felt a sense of relief I felt like I was free I could breathe again the days after that were extremely hard it was the beginning of my 3 week vacation I know it seems like I'm always on vacation but I always take off in the winter time. We continued to talk it's like I said I didn't think I was ready to let go and I thought maybe we could talk it out. Here I go being weak for this man again. That's why they say.. when you ask God for something.. you better be prepared for what he gives you or what he does for you. I was not prepared at all. He was like a drug that I was addicted to. One Morning he called and asked if I could pick him up and take him to his coworker's house so he catch a ride with him. It was early in the morning. I went to pick him up. We arrived at his coworker's house and coincidentally his coworker had already left for work. I asked, did you talk to your coworker? and he was like no. This man has a problem with just assuming people are always going to be there for him. With no effort on his part and this is how irresponsible he has always been. Just thinks people are magically going to show up for him. What's wrong with calling them and confirming? So now you got me out of my bed and for what? Now I had to bring him back to my house so he could catch an Uber to work.

That whole day I was thinking about him. I really can't let this dude go. Then it happened, and now I'm staying the night at his house. Nothing changed about us only his location. That first night I stayed at his house, was the best sex we had in years. So here I go being drawn in again the same week two days later I stayed the night again this time he asked me to take him to work in the morning. I guess I was so desperate to be in his presence that I agreed to it. Seven o'clock in the morning his phone rang. He sent it to voicemail. As soon as he got in the shower, I looked at his phone to see who called. It was a girl named Rashida. On the way to his job, I asked him if was he talking to someone or seeing anybody else. He stared into space before he answered me. He shook his head no. I already knew the answer but I guess since we were no longer a couple. I thought just maybe he would be honest with me for once. Then I said to him in the event that either one of us starts seeing other people I hope we can respect each other. He agreed. I just shook my head at him. During the day he called me to see if I could pick him up from work. This shit has to stop. I told him if I do I need gas money. I picked him up and dropped him back off at his house. He gave me the gas money and kissed me on the lips.

Then he immediately ran down to his cousin's house. He was in such a hurry. I could see him calling someone as he was walking extremely fast. This ninja thinks he's slick. I went home. The next night which was a Friday night He called me to see if I was still gonna stay the night. Of course, I am. This whole time I was OK with us no longer being a couple but still fucking like we use to. I was coming to terms with everything. I wasn't even thinking we were getting back together. I was enjoying the moment. However five minutes after I got to his house his phone rang. This Ninja did the 50-yard Dash to the bathroom with his phone. I thought that was kind of strange. So immediately I'm thinking is he talking to a female, of course, he's talking to a female. How dare he while I'm sitting here. So now I go to the bathroom and knock on the door, he yells to me don't come in here. I said what? You're crazy, why? So I went in there anyway I don't know what he did with the phone he must have put it behind his back I asked him was on the phone he said yes I'll be out in a minute oh now we're being secretive okay so, of course, he's talking to a female on the phone I go back to the room and I asked him what's going on why can't I come in the bathroom with you all of a sudden he gave me some spill about it's different now I said explain to me how it's different well when I was at your house you know that was our space and now it's just different now oh he said he wanted privacy why do you need privacy if I'm over here and I'm your company don't you think that's type rude? I told him I was leaving because I'm not beat for this bullshit. So go back and call whoever you were on the phone with. He said to me oh you're leaving. Now you're playing in my face I not gonna stay here and be DISRESPECTED. He apologized for being rude. Here I go again staying... got undressed and got in bed.

This mofo immediately started fucking me like he was super excited and super horny. I kept trying to get him to say my name and talk shit to me since he was pounding my pussy hard but he kept quiet. I said to myself yeah, he's seeing somebody. I waited for him to pass out as usual. Now I'm looking at the phone to see who it was that called when I first got there. Yeah, they say you females love to go to a brother's phone. Don't ever go through somebody's phone because nine times out of 10 you're going to find something.

I said Lord I know I didn't listen to you I was not prepared for you to take me out of this person's life I believe I'm ready now because he's still playing games he immediately went back to the way he was when I first met him. We are extremely too old for this foolishness I am in my fifties you are in your mid-40s what is the problem here? One problem is I have some insecurities I need to work out. Another issue is I have to let go and let God have it. Apparently, this day was not the day for that.

Chapter Ten

A Revaluation

This is the very last time that I go through the phone. The first time I went through his phone I opened Pandora's Box. This time when I went through the phone it was God telling me this is it. This is the mother of all mothers. If you do not leave this man alone... if this does not make you leave this man alone... This was God telling me I'm going to show you better than I can tell you I'm going to make sure you're ready to hear what I got to say to you, my child.

Have you ever wondered what your life would look like on the TV screen? Or maybe you felt like you were watching a movie instead of living in your own reality? This possibly could not be my life right now I'm watching everything play out right in front of me and I still don't believe what I just saw or heard. Not only did this man make a fool out of me time and time again but the playing in my face was the ultimate betrayal. I loved every bit of him through everything. I can't tell you how many times we spent at the hospital when he was having issues with his asthma. Every time he was sick, I was nurse Betty. Even when I didn't feel good, I took care of him. It's true what they say... Men are the worst babies when they get sick. I made sure he had what he needed. I made sure his son had what he needed. I'm not saying this to get any applause or to seem like I'm boasting. I'm simply saying I have no appreciation whatsoever. I did all I did just for this man to say I was never there for him. Although I try to live my life with no regrets he has really made me second guess that. I swear you do not know the true meaning of Devastation until you honestly go through it. God is speaking to me now I had to sit there and take my punishment for trying to love a narcissistic person. I didn't even know anything about narcissism until I went through what I went through. Before I get into all of that, this night has changed my life forever.

It is so hard for me to let people go. It takes them to let me go, for me to stop messing with them. Letting go was one of THE hardest lessons that I truly had to learn.

After he passed out sleep I went to the phone. Now during my investigation of the phone, I look to see who called him that Friday night when I got to his house. It was the same girl who had called him that Thursday Morning. Now I see the text messages between him and her. Apparently, she was over at his house the night before, which was Thursday night.

The same day that I took him to work. So let's recap... I stayed at his house Monday night, Wednesday night and Friday night. In the messages he's telling her, he messed up it should have been her all along. They're sending emojis back and forth □□□□❤

He's telling her he enjoyed kissing her all over last night. Kissing her neck and other places. She's telling HIM, I told my family all about you they can't wait to meet YOU. Prior to this, I had never heard of this girl I'd been going through his phone for years and never seen her at all. That is irrelevant right now. So here I am with his phone in my hand. I'm pacing the floor back and forth. I said Lord I know I have asked you time and time again to get me out of this situation, I am listening to you now. I will do what it takes to deliver me from this situation. Why am I not strong enough to just walk away? I have to make him be done with me. At that moment with his phone in my hand at 1:00 in the morning, I Dialed this person's number. She answered. I said hello this is Tina. She said oh I kind of figured that. How are you? Mind you, I'm calling from his phone. I said, I'm good and how are you? She said yeah he told me about you. Okay, so what about me? He told me y'all broke up like three weeks ago. Okay, that's sort of a true statement. But did he also tell you he was still seeing me? She said oh no, well thanks for telling me, she said. I see he has not changed. I said oh so how long y'all been talking? Apparently, he just hit her up after he left my house, three weeks ago. Her name is Rashida. She explained to me that they messed around maybe 10 years ago and the same scenario happened when some female called her about him. I spent at least an hour and a half on the phone with this girl. She gave me a lot of information. He's been telling her how he doesn't have a car because I took all his money. Basically telling her a whole bunch of Lies exaggerating the truth. Making it seem like I was a piece of shit. Telling her I had two grown kids who didn't help me in the house. Also, he had gotten a loan from his company so I could have the down payment to buy the house that we lived in. He told her it was $5,000 he got from his company which was only $3,500. He didn't know what I did with the money. The homeowner changed his mind about selling the house. So I spent the money on whatever needed to be paid for the house. Was I wrong for not telling him? Absolutely but I took out money here and there but I put it back. After the deal wasn't on the table anymore, I just kept spending the money until there was nothing left. Honestly, why should he know what I did with the money? He wasn't helping me pay anything in the house. That was the other lie he told her... That he had helped me pay for everything in the house. She asked him well who broke it off. Scrappy told her he got tired of it and he left. So he's making it seem like I'm not on top of my finances. That I dragged him down First of all he had nothing when I met him. He lived with his mother. Never had his own place nor paid any bills in his name except for the car he had. He barely had a job.

His credit score was in the toilet. After being with me he had calmed down a lot. Started working on his finances. Getting his credit score up to a decent number. it still wasn't anything to brag about but it was higher, he was getting better.

Rashida seemed to know a lot about what was going on in our relationship, for them to only have been talking for three weeks. That means every time y'all got on the phone it was about me. Gurl, that is definitely the first red flag. Rashida is about to step right into all his bullshit. And how does she not see that she is a just rebound? Then she proceeded to tell me that Scrappy wanted to buy a house with her. Plus once he got his income tax check he was going to pay to get her car out of the shop. Wooweee.. He's about to lay it on her thick. I was amazed at how I was keeping my cool during the whole conversation with her. The more she was telling me, the more my confirmation. I made up my mind right then and there. It was definitely time to leave this whole entire situation and leave that man alone. I knew this was it the moment I dialled her number. I began telling her everything that he did to me. She pretended to be disgusted by it and said she was going to block him. So we came up with a plan. I told her to call his phone at 7:00 in the morning like she normally does because I knew that was her the other morning. She said he's not going to answer if you're there. I said I know the first time he doesn't answer hang up and call right back. if he still doesn't answer I want you to call me on Facebook Messenger. She and I had already exchanged phone numbers but I wanted her to call me on messenger to make it look like she looked me up. Man, when I tell you this man was shaking when his phone rang. He immediately got up and started looking for something. I asked him what he was looking for. He told me that he was looking for the TV remote. I'm doing everything I can to keep my composure because the remote to the TV is sitting on top of his cell phone. His cell phone was sitting on the window ledge plugged into the charger. Once again his phone rang for the second time just as we had planned. Now he's sitting on the floor looking under the bed for the TV remote now I'm sitting up my phone rings I look at the picture on the phone and I start to say her name. This boy was waving to me like he was Landing a plane Then had the audacity to say, No don't answer that. He wanted me to be quiet. He wanted me not to answer MY PHONE. I said Man you TRIPPING, who the hell is? I answered. Rashida asked for him. I asked who is this? I was trying to see her name. But Scrappy snatched the phone from me. Now I'm yelling at him, give me my phone! and I snatched it back and I asked him well who was that? He tells me she's just a friend. I acted like I was pissed. I got dressed and left his house, hopped in my car and called Rashida back. She and I were cracking up. I know this is some high school shit... As I'm driving home still talking to her on the phone. Scrappy called me, but I didn't answer. So then he calls Rashida. She told me she'd call me back because she wanted to hear what he had to say. Even though Scrappy and I broke up, I felt like he was still playing games with me and I needed for it to stop. As long as he didn't have a car, he was still going to use me, while being with her. He basically wanted her but was still having sex with me. Once I saw the way he was moving or playing in my face, I had to be completely done. All he had to do was tell me the truth but that is something that did not exist in his whole entire being.

Once Rashida got off the phone with Scrappy, she called me. She says, Girl, he was on the phone crying talking about please give me another chance. I said he was crying. Like real tears? She said yes. Then he tells her, the reason why I came to his house last night was because I was begging him to get back with me. And I wanted to have sex with him one more time. Lord have mercy... The lies!!

She called him on three-way I sat there quietly as they talked Rashida was saying to him I told you not to play with me and I told you if you play with me what will happen. This grown man sat on the other end like a little boy who was getting scolded by his mother.

Sounding so pitiful adhering to her command. I sat there in disbelief. How is this the person that I just spent the last 5 years of my life with? Not only was he playing with me he was playing with her. She was just too blind to see it. She thought she had the upper hand over him. At the moment she did. He was sounding sad and pretended to be crying a little bit not realizing I was on the other end. So when he heard my voice on the other end it got real quiet. Then the ultimate betrayal came. I asked him why was he telling this girl all these lies about me. He said he didn't lie. Okay, so the real reason why I came over to your house last night was? His whole attitude changed at that moment. He went from being sad and pitiful to mad and angry. With such rage, he began to tell me to get off the phone. Then proceeded to say, oh your sister was right about you, You are crazy. He couldn't do anything else or say anything else all he did was hang up the phone. I'm sitting there laughing to myself. This boy is so full of it. Did he just discard me in front of this girl? This is not the same person I have known for the last 7 years. He's finally showing the real Timothy James Butler, a street Nigga from the hood. AKA "The Narcsists that I know."

Although this boy has not been diagnosed as being a narcissist. We have definitely gone through the stages that suggest narcissistic behaviour. During the love bomb stage, he had me in a triangular situation, third-party energy. Then the devaluation stage where he had me feeling like I wasn't good enough. I was begging for sex. I was still loving him, tending to him, catering to him while he would breadcrumb me with his sex. I watched him self-sabotage himself, damn near self-destruct. Go through a state of depression.

Just being angry at everything and everybody. Acting like a baby. Playing the victim of the circumstances that he created time and time and time again. I even watched him go through a semi-healing. I knew God told me it was time. There was nothing else I could do for this person. There was nothing else that I needed to learn from this person. So I ended our relationship. What I have learned about narcissistic people is once you leave them alone, you hurt their feelings. Once you hurt their feelings they will do everything in their power to destroy you. When he told me he was moving out I did not try to stop him I did not beg him to stay I told him it was messed up how he went about it but I completely understood and it was for the best I had no ill feelings about it. It wasn't until we decided to keep seeing each other, that things went completely wrong. But they were necessary. It had to go down that. So it could align me to what was my next chapter.

So I thought once he gave me the discard that would have been the end. It was not the end of my lessons with this person or in life.

After the 3-way call Rashida and I continued to talk later on that day she texted me and asked me why was I reaching out to her ex-boyfriend and telling him the situation that was going on between her and my ex meaning Scrappy I was completely taken back by this conversation first of all I don't know her nor do I know her ex-boyfriend. I know nothing about this girl. Then she sends a screenshot of a message supposedly her ex-boyfriend sent her of an alleged conversation between him and I. This ratchet chick took my Facebook profile picture and attached it to some text messages appearing to be from Facebook Messenger. The message was so stupid and the way it was worded, I do not talk like that.

I am not ghetto! Plus I had a different name on Facebook. I would not address myself by that name to people on a personal level. First of all, who does that? Who makes up Fake Messages? Rashida said no need for us to continue talking then she blocked me.

Apparently, I was still being naive in believing in people and their intentions. Here I am basically giving her the 411 to walk away not because I wasn't done dealing with him I really was done dealing with him. But girl go save yourself. Instead of her taking heed to that, I came across as being a liar. So she could no longer be associated with me because she still wanted to fuck him.

Chapter Eleven

The Drama Continues

I did not have a problem being blocked by this new chick. I didn't even have a problem with Scrappy blocking me. I did however have a problem with Scrappy's daughter blocking me. She felt as though all I wanted to do was talk about her dad. She told if she and I couldn't have our own relationship, then she didn't want to talk to me. That was fine but then she turned around and blocked me too. I was feeling some sort of way about that. That was the one thing that hurt my feelings. Because I had a close relationship with both of his kids I did nothing wrong to this man. So I had to swallow my pride on that one.

Monday Morning Comes Around Scrappy calls me. He asked me why did I tell Rashida that he gave me an STD. Wow, this chick is so full of shit just like him. This is the second lie this chick has told On Me. Now it was becoming clear why his daughter blocked me.

This man had a history of exaggerating the truth or just plain flat-out lying. So it's no wonder that he lied about how things occurred and how things took place, made me look like I was the worst person in the world. Just a cover of all the stuff that he did to me and for some new pussy. Now this new chick Rashida, she got a taste of the dick and how good the dick was. So she didn't want to let that go. So her plan was to tell lies to me to make sure that Scrappy wouldn't come back to me. Little did she know she did not have to go through all of that because as time went on she would see that I was not the threat and that other people would be involved in this man. He has not changed. He might have changed his location and the way he moved. But he has not taken the time to do the work to better himself. He was a habitual liar, a cheater and a master manipulator. That's something you do not change overnight. She thinks just because she put a locator on his phone and got the keys to his room, yes room because he does not own his own house nor does he rent his own apartment.

He rents a room and has a roommate. How do I know all of this you ask, if I was blocked by all of these people? Because both of them kept this stuff going, I blocked all of them on my phone but the way my phone is set up I can see who tried to text and call me it goes to a spam folder. One afternoon February 24th to be exact, one week after the last night I spent with Scrappy, I saw Rashida trying to text me. The text read "Why are you so concerned if your ex is still talking to me or not"? I read the text and I laughed I'm like what is this chick talking about I have not talked to this person in days so where is this coming from? I chose to ignore it. A few moments later she texted again… "why are you still talking to my ex and telling him everything that's going on between me and your ex if y'all want to talk to one another that's fine leave me and Scrappy out of it don't worry about me and Scrappy". Wait a minute, what do you mean don't worry about you and Scrappy? Oh, so y'all together now? That's what I said in my mind but now I'm getting pissed off because you have the audacity to think you're doing something by trying to check me with your lies? So now I called the chick. First of all girl, I'm going to tell you this one last time… I do not know your ex I don't give a fuck about you or Scrappy! Y'all want to be together then fucking go be together leave me the fuck alone! She then says I just want to know why you keep texting my ex? OH MY GOD! First of all, I don't have his NUMBER. How the hell would I text him? She said not his phone number was on the messenger. Now I know you lying because I deleted my Facebook two weeks ago so come again BITCH. She OH! Yeah, OH BITCH! Why don't you call your ex while I'm on the phone right now let's get to the bottom of this. She says oh you want me to call him? That's what the fuck I said Bitch! Then she pretended that someone was talking to her in the background so she said oh well let me call you right back. Yeah, you do that! 10 minutes later Scrappy texts me. Throughout our whole relationship, he has never called me out of my name. Now this man, this little boy proceeds to text me... look bitch I'm trying to be nice leave me and my girl alone before something bad happens to you and I won't regret it. I said these people are sick they are sick what the fuck is going on here? Now I'm about to take my earrings off and get me some Vaseline type of situation going on here, no lie. They really want me to get out of character so I can look crazy, they almost got me.

I called Scrappy and asked him what the hell he was talking about. He says he saw the text messages between me and her ex-boyfriend I said I started yelling at him... I'm going to tell you like I told her I do not know her ex-boyfriend. So you couldn't have possibly seen no message between him and I. This girl is doing what she can because she's so worried about you coming back to me, she trying to make it seem like I'm doing all of this and that to make sure that you won't fuck with me no more it's too bad that you don't fucking see that. I don't give a fuck about you or her. You made your choice you made your decision and I have accepted that You want to be with her. Go fucking be with her and leave me the fuck alone! He didn't say one word. He sat there and listened to everything I said. He knew he was completely wrong. But guess what, now you got to stand on it, Bro! Fuck You and your bullshit ass threats. And fuck her!

Days ahead I believe I was still in shock about what had transpired. I still had to come to the revaluation of that chapter of my life has ended. And that I deserved more or better out of a relationship. When I tell you I went through so many emotions in the next month it was still unbelievable to me I have only been in two serious relationships my whole life I have lived with two men who didn't fully respect me not only as a person or as their significant other. I was beginning to realize that I had a pattern of choosing people. For the most part, I loved it out of convenience. When I was with my daughter's father it was just convenient for us to live together because I didn't have my shit together. When Scrappy and I lived together it was out of convenience because he was displaced out of his home and he didn't have his shit together. So now I'm sitting here trying to put myself back together realizing that I really don't know who I am. Because I allowed myself to live for everyone else instead of living for me. I started to try to clutch onto people. Doing anything to get this hurt from me. I just wanted to be around anyone. It seemed like every door kept getting slammed in my face. I didn't know how to handle being hurt I didn't know how to move forward I spent all this time trying to please everyone else I didn't know what I needed for myself I just kept running and running and running it was like I was running a race, a race to find comfort in the familiar. It got to the point where, you know how you would Shake somebody because they're acting irrational or slapped them across the face to snap out of it? Well, I got punched in my chest so hard it made me stop. It was God saying if you don't sit down and be still. Just sit down you have to be still. I am going to pull you through this. You have to allow me to pull you through this.

You were not made to be broken!

Chapter Twelve

Time To Heal

I started a new Facebook page because I deleted my previous one. Upon opening this page, these videos for Narcsists started popping up. As I said earlier, I never knew anything about A narcissist. This started my healing Journey. The more I started to watch these videos it became very clear that the person that I was involved with was very much a narcissistic person. The more that I started to be in tune with myself, things started to come to the forefront without me manifesting anything. This let me know that I was on the right path to healing and that God was on my side. I was definitely getting closer to God. Not only did those videos start popping up all these other videos of songs that I needed to hear popped up as well. They definitely helped me during my healing journey. They also helped me get ideas for my new page. The next thing I knew, I started getting a lot of followers. It was so surreal. Even though it felt good it was scary at the same time. Now I'm paying more attention to my spirit and what God is trying to show me. For the most part, I am learning. I am seeing you for the first time in my life. I am no longer thinking of feeding My Flesh. Scrappy was the last person to feed my flesh. I don't know if I'll ever be with someone again but right now that's not important to me. What is important to me is to get closer to God and to live a healthier life. One thing I recently discovered was that I am sensitive to chemicals, adjectives, and processed food.

I pretty much thought I should live in a bubble with all the things that I'm allergic to. Now not only do I have to watch what I eat or put on my skin, I also have to watch what I put in my spirit.

There are so many life coaches or counsellors that are online now. I didn't search for anyone in particular somehow these people found me. I would log on to Facebook and click on the reels and every reel that came up was pertaining to whatever I was thinking about on that day or what I have been going through. I was just amazed. Somehow this app can tell you what you should be learning for the day. Throughout this whole journey, things have just been coming to me and I had to realize they have been coming to me all my life I just haven't been paying that close attention. Now I'm learning things that I need to work on to be a better person. Sometimes I would get triggered by thinking of what I just went through. That was definitely something that I was working on. Finding out why am I being triggered by that certain thing. There were so many things I have learned on this journey, that I don't think I would have learned if I was still with Scrappy.

Or still sitting in that situation that no longer served me. There was no room for growth in that relationship for either one of us. I have discovered that I have codependency and abandonment issues. Meaning that I felt the great need to take care of everyone else not realizing that I was hurting myself in the process. Somehow that was making me feel whole. As long as I could give people unconditional love, I felt good about myself. Not realizing that gave them the power to use me. I had a hard time standing up for myself or saying no to people. Because I feared losing them or them walking out on me. That's when the abandonment issues came in, I did not know that I had these issues. Although these people might have been broken in their own way, I did not know I too was broken.

That's why it was so easy for people to manipulate me. They always say that you may have childhood trauma that you need to deal with before you can move on. Well, apparently my childhood issues of codependency and abandonment led my inner child to be resentful. I don't feel like I'm resentful I thought I dealt with everything that I needed to throughout my life but apparently, I didn't. That's how I allowed all bullshit to go on in my life. Now that I know that, I can correct that problem. Too many of us are walking around unhealed.

That's why there are so many Narcissistic people in this world. At some point, I said, Damn am I the narcissist? I definitely exhibited some of that behaviour. I've been around too many and didn't know that I picked up some of their traits. Whatever is wrong, I'm taking accountability and correcting it. I'm not shifting the blame on anyone.

This is my life it's time to get it together.

I have learned that you need discernment in order to move forward. I took accountability for everything that I did in this relationship, accountability for hurting my own heart I saw the red flags I saw that he was no good I made a conscious decision to stand by him. I truly hurt myself in this situation and fell back further than I needed to be from my purpose in life. It was absolutely my fault. I accepted him for who he was and expected him to love me the way that I loved him. Only to realize you can't make a person be ready for what they are not ready for. Or to love you the way that you love them. He didn't love himself. So how could he love me? Self-consciously I was trying to change him without Really Trying to change him, if that makes sense. I didn't look at it as though I was trying to change him I just wanted him to wake up one day and choose me. After fighting for so long for him to choose me I finally realized that it cannot be done. He has to do it on his own. I can't force him I may have given up on him but I didn't give up on me. I lost myself trying to be everything for him. Now it was time to find me again or to embrace a new version of me. It's gonna take time. I have to give myself grace, patience and understanding. Lord knows this journey is not easy but it is so worth it.

Months have gone by. I felt like things were starting to get better and brighter. After I had that one big cry, the anger and disappointment set in. I was more disappointed in myself. I had to forgive myself for allowing it to go on like it did. One day I was cleaning out my dining room closet. There were all these boxes in there that I had forgotten about. They belonged to Scrappy. There were a lot of summer clothes in there. My first thought was to just throw everything out. Which I should have done. But then I thought maybe he might need this stuff. I called him and left him a voice message since he still had me blocked. I informed him that they were there and if I didn't hear from him by that Wednesday then that Thursday, I'll put them out to be picked up on trash day. I didn't hear from him I still left them in there when Thursday came around. I didn't put it out to be picked up. Since I had him block, I didn't think to check my SPAM folder. Friday afternoon I checked my spam folder and saw that he tried to call me four times Friday morning I told myself I was not going to call him back I was feeling strong and confident about myself so it was no big deal to me at that time. However, something told me that he was just going to pop up after he got off of work. I just had that feeling. Lo and behold later on that evening I was sitting on my front porch a car pulled up in front of my house and it was Scrappy. He had his passenger side window rolled down and he started to yell out to me. But then he decided to park he walked up to my front porch. I looked at him with this disgusted look. I thought to myself... how dare you pull up here unannounced! This was the first time I had seen him since the last time we had sex. I kept my composure though. He walked up to the gate and asked very softly, "You said you had some things for me?" I honestly didn't know what to say to him I was having a discussion in my head about what to say and how to react I just shook my head yes and told him to come inside. He came inside. I didn't ask him anything about the situation he had going on. He asked me how I've been.

I told him I'm doing great. He went through the things and said he was only taking certain things I told him to take all of it. What you decide to do with them once they leave my house is your business. Don't leave your trash in my house. He picked his stuff up and put it in his car. I said, oh I'm glad you have a car now. He said yes, it's not much but it's to get me to and from where I need to go. I said that's good that's a good start I guess that gave him the initiative to tell me what was going on in his house or what he had going on as far as his finances. He was talking to me like nothing ever happened. You were sent to try to destroy me and now you're in my face acting like that nothing ever happened? This was the problem with us all the time. We would fight and then 2 minutes later it's like the fight never happened. His own son said that to me, he doesn't understand us. We can have a whole brawl not that we did, but if we damn near kill each other, 2 minutes later we're back playing nice. That was always funny to me because it was the truth. We have always been that way I can't understand it I can't explain it we can make each other mad as hell but then go right back to being friends again. Before he left to get back in his car, I said take care of yourself. I showed no emotion to this person whatsoever. His response was I'm going to try. I said

OKAY and I waved. Then he starts talking again telling me about other people in his life and I'm looking at him like I really don't want to hear this just take your stuff and go. Then I said, okay goodbye. He says okay I'll talk to you later, as if we will talk again. I just shook my head and went back into the house. Who does this guy think he is? Nevertheless, I felt good for standing my ground. I didn't owe him anything. I didn't owe him my conversation, my kindness or my generosity. If I owed him anything that would have been for me not to open the door! That was fine, I let it go.

Five months after we broke up I was starting to feel better about myself. Then all of a sudden it was like I couldn't get him off my mind. I had this great need to have a conversation with him it was so strong I said here I go again why do I feel like this because every time I felt like this I had to call him. Here he is hindering my spirit once again I don't want to be with him this has gone on for I don't know how long now. it's starting to really bother me why can't I shake this person out of my system? It seemed that whatever I was doing was not working. So I consulted a psychic medium. I got a reading and I had to ask her why do I keep thinking about my ex. I don't want him back but why do I keep thinking about him? Her response was, you keep thinking about him because he's your twin flame. I'm sorry, my what? She said your twin flame, so you're always going to be connected. You two were supposed to hurt one another because you both needed to learn some lessons. You were supposed to part ways. Once you both have evolved separately, you will be together again. However, in order for your Divine Masculine or life partner to heal... You as the Divine Feminine have to heal first. Then he will start his healing process. Now I have to look up the word twin flame because I didn't know anything about it. I did believe her as far as us still being connected. My question is, how is this Narcissistic person My Divine Masculine after all the Demonic things I witnessed? He has Hella soul ties that can't be erased. I'm no angel nor am I perfect but Lord I guess I am gonna have to trust you on this one. This is crazy because in my reality he gave me a false reality. I was being real and he perceived it to be fake. We did mirror one another. It's like Good Angel vs. Bad Angel. I am the light full of love and he is the darkness full of mischievous ways. No matter how you look at we are one of the same.

Until we meet again, My Narcsistic toxic, Twin Flame.

BIO

Inspiring Writer, on the path that God has led me. My main focus is to help bring Love back into the world through my books. What is Love? So many of us honestly don't know how to love. Or what to do in Love. My stories are based on true stories but are told in a fictitious way. Before we love anyone, we must first love ourselves. We start by asking God for clarity so he can guide us in the right direction. Love is what we do. For I Am Love.

Special Acknowledgements

I would like to dedicate this book to my children. If we don't have anything else in this world, we have each other and God. He is always on our side. Special dedication to my Aunt Diane for always being there. Also to my Soul Sister Tye AKA Barbie Twin, much love girl.

www.ingramcontent.com/pod-product-compliance
Lightning Source LLC
LaVergne TN
LVHW011050110826
845149LV00015B/3435

* 9 7 8 1 9 6 2 8 8 6 2 0 8 *